Rita and
the Romans

Also by Hilda Offen:

Rita on the River

Rita Rides Again

Rita and the Flying Saucer

RITA THE RESCUER

Rita and the Romans

Hilda Offen

troika books

For Lily Cox

Published by TROIKA BOOKS

First published 2017

1 3 5 7 9 10 8 6 4 2

Text and illustrations copyright © Hilda Offen 2017

The moral rights of the author/illustrator have been asserted

A CIP catalogue record for this book is available from the British Library

ISBN 978-1-909991-55-2

Printed in Poland

Troika Books
Well House, Green Lane, Ardleigh CO7 7PD, UK

www.troikabooks.com

"It's Roman Day at the Sports Field!" said
Julie. "I'm going to the mosaic class."

"I'm a trumpeter," said Jim.

"And I'm the Standard Bearer for the
Roman army!" said Eddie.
"We've got a giant catapult.
We're going to fight the Picts."

"Can I come?" asked Rita.

"No!" said Eddie. "You haven't got a costume."

"I have! I have!" cried Rita. "I've got a toga in my dressing-up box. Please wait for me!"

"Not likely!" said Eddie.

They pulled the garden roller across the Wendy-house door and ran off to the Sports Field.

Rita pushed and
pushed but the door
wouldn't budge.
"Huh!" she thought.
"It's a good thing I've
got my Rescuer outfit
here."

Rita was so furious that she changed
in double-quick time. Then she dived
at the floor, whirring round and
round like a drill. She burst out
through a flower-bed and headed for
the Sports Field.

The mosaic class was in uproar.

"It's those jackdaws from the castle ruins!" said the teacher. "They keep stealing the blue bits!"

"Leave it to me," said Rita. She flew to the top of the castle. "You should be ashamed of yourselves!" she said to the jackdaws.

"Sorry!" they squawked. "Blue's our favourite colour."

"And what's this shiny bird?" asked Rita.

We found it – honest!

Rita tucked the bird in her belt and flew
back with the mosaic pieces.

"Oh, thank you Rescuer!" cried the teacher.
"Now we can get on."

"And so can I!" said Rita. She could hear
someone nearby, puffing and blowing like a
walrus. It was Adrian Oakley, the builder.

"What's up?" asked Rita.

"I've promised to build this wall in time for the battle," puffed Mr Oakley. "But the blocks are too heavy. I'm not going to get it done."

"Cheer up, Mr Oakley!" said Rita. "I'll help you."

"Oh thanks, Rescuer!" said Mr Oakley. "And please – call me Adrian."

"Right-ho, Adrian!" said Rita, "Let's get to work on this wall."

They were finished in no time.

"That should keep the Picts out," said Rita.

"Uh-oh! Time to go!"

Someone was roaring "YOU'VE DONE WHAT?"

A Roman Centurion was glaring at Eddie.

"What do you mean, you've 'lost the eagle'?" he roared.

"It must have dropped off," said Eddie.

"We can't go into battle without our eagle!" shouted the Centurion.

"Is this what you're looking for?" asked
Rita. "I found it in a jackdaw's nest."
"Phew!" said Eddie. "Thanks, Rescuer."

"Romans! Forward march!" roared the Centurion. "Man the catapult!"

The Picts were really the local cricket team. They peeped over the wall and stuck out their tongues.

No-one noticed a toddler climbing into the catapult.

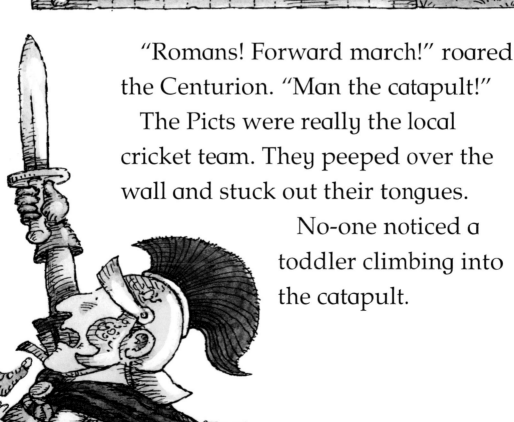

"Load the ammunition!" cried the Centurion. "Fire!"
The crowd gasped.

"Oh dear!" said the Centurion as the toddler whizzed overhead. "Oh dear!"

But Rita had seen what was happening.
She shot through the air and caught the
toddler in the nick of time.

"Well held!" cried the Picts.

Oh—
thank you,
Rescuer!

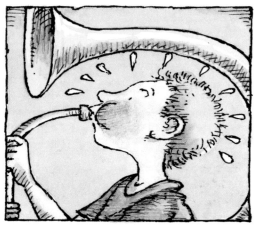

"Time for the Chariot Race!" cried the announcer.

It was Jim's big moment. He raised his trumpet and blew. Nothing happened. He blew and he blew but not a sound came out.

"Let's see what I can do!" said Rita.

She gave an enormous puff – and out shot a potato! TAA-RAA! went the trumpet – and the race was on!

Round and round the course thundered the chariots, pulled by the two fittest ponies in the pony club.

All at once the crowd caught its breath.
A little girl had wandered on to the track!
"She'll be trampled!" they cried.
But Rita had seen the danger.

She swooped down and snatched the little girl from under the ponies' hooves.

"Hello, Rescuer!" said the little girl. "Would you like a daisy?"

"Oh – thanks!" said Rita.

Below them the ponies thundered over the finishing line and everyone cheered.

"Now – the moment you've been waiting for!" cried the announcer. "Here come the Gladiators!"

A lion and a gladiator ran into the arena and saluted each other. Then the fight began.

They were interrupted by a savage howl as
Basher Briggs and his dog burst from the crowd.
"Go on, Monster, grab'em!" yelled Basher.
"I'm off!" whimpered the gladiator.
"Rip!" The lion costume tore apart.
The front legs went one way and
the back legs the other.

Rita ran into the arena and whispered in Monster's ear. He stopped barking and rolled on his back while Rita tickled his tummy.
Then he ran off into the crowd.

"Basher! You need a lesson!" said Rita.
She speared Basher's cap with the trident
and threw the net over him.

"Hooray!" yelled the crowd.

"Hooray for the Rescuer!"

"Shall I let him go or hook him on the flagpole?" Rita asked.

The crowd gave the thumbs-down sign.

"Hook him on the flagpole!" they roared. So Rita did.

Then Rita entered some competitions. She guessed the number of pickled walnuts, she won the javelin contest and she defeated the champion wrestler.

After that she entered the Public Speaking Competition. She told some good jokes and made everyone laugh; and she said a few thoughtful things, too.

"Well done, Rescuer!" said the mayor.
"You're the winner!"
"Oh, thank you!" said Rita. "I'm honoured!"
And she flew away over the Sports Field
and back to the Wendy-house.

It wasn't long before Eddie, Julie and Jim came rushing down the path. They pulled away the roller.

"Sorry, Rita!" said Jim. "You've missed the Rescuer again – she was amazing."

"We've got you some honeycakes," said Julie. "And a snake bracelet – it's meant to bring you luck."

"Thank you!" said Rita. "If it works, I might even get to see the Rescuer one day."

Look out for other Rita titles from Troika Books

Rita and the Flying Saucer

When a group of Aliens from Planet Norma Alpha cause
trouble Rita has to call on all her special powers. She
smashes an asteroid, returns a lost Norm to his flying saucer
and then shows the visitors the way home through space.

Rita Rides Again

Whether it's ghosts in the castle,
monsters in the moat or a flock
of angry peacocks, you can count
on the Rescuer!

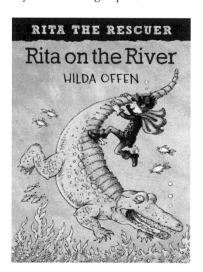

Rita on the River

Rita rescues a puppy that can't swim,
assists an island castaway and saves
some swimmers from a giant crocodile
about to open its fearsome jaws!